by P. Ryan Rooney
illustrated by Sue Cornelison

To contact the author, Patty Rooney:

pryanrooney@hotmail.com

or visit her website at **www.pryanrooney.com**

To contact the illustrator, Sue Cornelison:

sfc.illustration@gmail.com

or visit her website at **www.suecornelison.com**

Copies of this book are available from the author or illustrator or online.

Library of Congress PCN: 2016917176

ISBN-13: 97809979841-3-2

ISBN-10: 09979841-3-9

WWW.ZIONPUBLISHING.ORG
Zion Publishing
Des Moines IA

Published in the United States of America

For all little girls
of every age...

P. R.R.

S.F.C.

Not really very long ago,
Although it seems that way.
A little girl who had no curls
Sat 'neath a tree one day.

This little girl had lost her smile
because she had no friend.
But suddenly, behind the tree,
A voice said, "My name's Whim."

She turned around to face the sound;
She didn't trust her eyes.
She closed them tight, but still saw light,
A glorious surprise!

He had a very happy face
And flimsy see-through wings
That fluttered like a butterfly,
And on his toes were rings.

She could almost see right through him.
In disbelief she said,
"I must be just imagining.
You must be in my head."

"Oh, silly little girl," he said,
"I'm here to see you through
And when you're grown and on your own
You still might need me too.

You never have to be alone,
Just close your eyes to see.
If you will think, then in a wink,
You'll have a friend in me."

He handed her a ring to wear;
It took away her fear.
She floated there—right in mid-air
Her sadness disappeared!

She clapped her hands and squealed with joy,
"Oh, Whim, what shall we do?"
"The choice is yours, then we'll explore.
It all depends on you."

"You think that we could walk on clouds?
Oh, can we do that, Whim?"
"We'll take a spoon and taste the moon
And then come back again."

She followed him through outer space.
They plucked some lucky stars.
She laughed when Whim tried juggling them
And dropped them all on Mars.

They laughed and danced and sang off key,
They didn't walk; they'd run!
They yelled real loud; they bounced on clouds.
She'd never had such fun.

They used a rainbow as a slide and landed at the tree.

The sun was down which made her frown. "So now, you're going to leave?"

Her eyes began to make some tears
But no, she shook her head.
"Where will you go? I need to know.
Where will you make your bed?"

Whim looked around to find a place
That he could call his own.
“This tree will give some space to live;
It’s where I’ll make my home."

"I think this tree will work," she said.
"In fact, I think it's fine.
She hugged the tree for Whim to see—
Declared it, “yours and mine."

They carved their names and wrote the date.
They marked how tall they were.
They struck a deal that made it real
Forever: Whim and her.

And all was fine as they shook hands
And stepped back to survey.
"This little space shall be our place.
We'll meet here every day."

Whim

Each day was an adventure then.
She never did get bored.
They'd search for gold; be pirates bold,
Or royalty, "M'Lord."

Sometimes, their tree would be an isle
With them shipwrecked at sea.
Or they might hide 'til gangsters spied
Them crouching in their tree.

And so they met for many years. And oh, what times they had.

As long as Whim was her best friend, then nothing else was bad.

But as the girl began to grow,
She'd miss a day or two.
And though she'd yearn, she had to learn
Important things—at school.

She didn't visit by and by
And when one day she came.
It worried Whim to see her then.
She didn't seem the same.

He strained his neck to see her face.
He really should have known.
He checked the bark and then remarked,
"Oh, my, how you have grown."

He seemed a little nervous when
He asked her, "Shall we play?"
She hung her head, and simply said,
"Not now, Whim. Not today."

"Well, I guess I'd better go now…
There's not much more to say…
There's nothing new for us to do…
I will come back… some day."

Whim scratched his head in thoughtful thought,
Deciding what to say,
"If you will think, then in a wink,
I'll help you find the way."

And Whim was of the loyal sort,
As loyal as can be.
Though seasons passed, he stood by fast
And waited by their tree.

And even though Whim stayed the same,
The little girl did not.
She grew and grew as girls will do
And so, she changed a lot.

She was a woman, not a girl;
Time had finally caught her.
She had become someone else's mom—
A baby girl, her daughter.

She worried more and giggled less,
Her smile was lost again.
Her childish dreams were gone, it seemed,
She rarely thought of Whim.

She had a furrow in her brow,
Familiar with regret.
Her duties loomed; she felt consumed—
Her daughter felt neglect.

One day, with so much work to do…
A deadline… bills to send…
Her daughter sighed, and finally cried,
"Mommy, I have no friend."

Her heart was pierced with memories
Of days that she once knew.
She thought of Whim; because of him
She knew just what to do.

She took her daughter by the hand.
The "real world" set to "pause."
"Let's take a walk and have a talk
Right now and just because…

"I love you very much," she said,
"And so to prove it true,
Because I care I'm going to share
That I was young once, too.

"There's something I will give you first;
It's something we must bring."
She searched around until they found
A tarnished friendship ring.

"This ring is yours to wear and keep;
It's from a precious friend.
His name is Whim—when you meet him
He'll help your sadness end."

They walked and talked and finally stopped
And sat beneath a tree.
The small girl's eyes were filled with 'whys?'
But Mom said, "Wait and see."

And side by side they sat as time
Seemed very slow to pass.
And like a worm, the small one squirmed,
When suddenly, she gasped,

"Oh, Mommy! Look!" her daughter squealed.
"It's him! Can you see him?"
She realized her daughter's eyes
Were focused in on Whim.

She did not see though sensed him near.
And knew she always would.
She also knew, as her heart grew
That now her daughter could.

The little girl ran off with Whim
To laugh and play a while.
The grown up girl who had no curls
Sat 'neath the tree and smiled.

On a Whim—The Story Behind the Story

Whim is always here whenever we pay attention.

With three little girls all under the age of three, my experience of the early 1980's was a blur, living in a perpetual state of exhaustion. One day, while taking a rare, quiet shower, these words came to me, "Oh silly little girl," he said, "I'm here to see you through. And when you're grown and on your own, you still might need me too."

Having no idea what it meant, or who "he" was, still wrapped in a towel and dripping wet, I wrote down the words. This became a frequent scenario; inspiration, it seems, does not concern itself with timing. Slowly and surely, the story began to unfold and I became acquainted with Whim. I wrote his story and then tucked Whim away, thinking that the story would be something I could give to my daughters someday. Still, I also hoped to find an illustrator who could bring my friend to life. For nearly thirty years, whenever I was in a bookstore, I looked through children's books, searching for an illustrator who could capture Whim. Nothing.

Fast forward to 2013. I received a magazine I had never received before (or since). Usually such mail never enters my house, but on a whim, just before pitching it into the recycling bin, I opened it to a page that stopped me in my tracks: a gorgeous painting that was exactly what I had been searching for lo, these many years. The artist's name—Sue Cornelison. Her work—described as "Whimsical"! And she lived only 40 minutes away!

I began what could probably be considered stalking her until we finally met. Sue and I worked off and on and in and around our lives for about three years until Whim was born.

With Sue and I nearing the final stages of the book, on a whim, I mentioned our idea to a friend who said, "You should talk to Mary Nilsen of Zion Publishing."

I believe that Whim gathered us together, and when the three of us met, Team Whim was complete. We are happy to introduce you to him and hope that you will introduce Whim to your children and grandchildren.

Patty Ryan Rooney

Thank you for reading this book.

We are hoping you will spread the story of ***Whim***.

Here's how:

Log into Amazon.com and write a review of ***Whim*** so that other mothers and grandmothers and everyone who loves children will be encouraged to buy a copy.

Hard cover copies are available for $18.95
Soft cover copies are available for $9.95 at:
www.pryanrooney.com
www.suecornelison.com
online or at a bookstore near you.

The lazer-printed hard cover book makes a beautiful gift.

Share the spirit of Whim.

64145922R00021

Made in the USA
Charleston, SC
19 November 2016